D1120127

To a strawbeater, Louise Godfrey McNeil, who taught me
"I love you, Black Child"
I. S.

To my mother, for just being there

And for Bruce and Charlotte Nesbitt
Thank you for helping to make it happen.
M. B. R.

First Edition

Principal Sources
Abrahams, Roger D. *Singing the Master.* New York: Pantheon, 1972. Barrow, David C. "A Georgia Corn Shucking." *Century* 24 (1882): 873–878. Jackson, Bruce, editor. *The Negro and His Folklore in 19th-Century Periodicals.* Austin: University of Texas Press, American Folklore Society, 1967.

Library of Congress Cataloging-in-Publication Data

Smalls-Hector, Irene.
  A strawbeater's thanksgiving / by Irene Smalls ; illustrated by Melodye Benson Rosales. — 1st ed.
    p. cm.
  Summary: Determined to be the strawbeater during the corn shucking party, Jess, a small young slave boy, wrestles a bigger, stronger boy for the honor.
  ISBN 0-316-79866-5
  [1. Determination (Personality trait) — Fiction. 2. Slavery — Fiction. 3. Afro-Americans — Fiction.] I. Rosales, Melodye, ill. II. Title.
  PZ7.S63915St 1998
  [E] — dc21   97-11711

10 9 8 7 6 5 4 3 2 1

SC

Published simultaneously in Canada by Little, Brown & Company (Canada) Limited

Printed in Hong Kong

AUTHOR'S NOTE

This story is based on slave narratives describing corn shuckings, which celebrated the harvest and were usually held in late November. Shucks were the principal source of food for cattle during the winter and were used by slaves in making toys, dolls, and straw hats, as stuffing for bedding, as wicks for lamps, and for medicine.

A strawbeater is a musician who stands behind a fiddler, reaches around his left shoulder, and beats on the strings while the fiddle is being played, in the manner of a snare drum.

It was late November, and the harvesting was done. With the overseer at the front of the line, the slaves made their way to the fields. There they pulled the cornstalks, throwing them into wagons that would take them to the corn shucking. The slaves' voices rose and fell with the movement of their hands: "Come day, go day, God send Sunday."

Jess, a young boy, and Sis Wisa, his mother, an older slave, were working the trash gang. The trash gang — bellied women, the old, and the young — cleaned up after the main work crew.

Sis Wisa uneasily pulled the loose bits of corn straw and beat them down into her basket. She glanced at Jess. *My last baby has high ideas,* she thought. *Gon be somebody, maybe head of the work gang or someday see the freedom sun shine.*

Jess enviously eyed Nathaniel, a large boy near the front.

"I'm seven and 'most a man," Jess puffed, flexing a small arm.

Then he scampered back to his task, singing, "Slip shuck corn little while, little while, I say."

As he bent over the cornstalks, he called out, "Mama, this time I want to be Ole Fiddler's strawbeater."

Sis Wisa laughed. "Chile, you kick the sweetening out of a ginger snap."

Jess held out a pair of straws. Using the air as his fiddle, he played the straws like drumsticks, humming along: "Tum tee tum. Tum tee tum."

Up ahead, Nathaniel noticed what Jess was doing and hurried to the back of the line to make that little boy stop pretending to do what Nathaniel knew was his job.

Nathaniel lumbered up. "Jess, you can't be no strawbeater. Why, I always been the strawbeater, and I will be again." The hulking boy pushed Jess hard and then moved on.

Jess hurled back, "I'se gon be strawbeater!"

Jess went back to work before the overseer could see him dawdling. He looked up at his mother. "Mama, do you think I could be Fiddler's strawbeater?"

"What do you think, Jess?"

"Well, I thinks I can."

"Then you can," she answered.

"Mama, tell me agin 'bout the corn shucking," Jess said.

"The general gives out the song," Sis Wisa replied, "and the workers answer with the refrain and shuck. They git the hog bladders blowed full of air and hold them in the fire, and they go pop pop pop."

"They is goin' to be jig dancing — the pigeon wing, too," Jess added excitedly.

As the sun set, the horn blew. The slaves trudged back to the quarter.

Finally, the evening of the corn shucking arrived. After a full day in the fields, the harvest moon shining brightly, Jess, Sis Wisa, Nathaniel, and a group of the others set off. Some of them carried pine torches. Farmers along the way had set raw buckets of tar afire. The night blazed with bright pits of light. Sis Wisa had taken her hair down out of its many colored strings. In the crowd there was a ribbon here, a new hat there.

They joined slaves coming from farms all over. The groups walked carefully past the patrollers, the armed gangs of men that kept watch over the roads between the farms. The corn shucking meant that the farmers would be ready for winter earlier. The patrollers let the slaves pass.

Jess's group arrived just as the fence rail was being set atop the mountainous corn pile, dividing it in two. This was accompanied by much wrangling. Once the fence rail was set, shuckers were divided into two groups. Two corn generals were chosen to lead the opposing sides. Nathaniel made sure he was on the side opposite Jess.

Thaddeus, corn general for Jess's side, called from the top of Corn Mountain, an ear of corn in each hand, "Here is yer corn shucker."

"Oh ho ho ho ho ho ho ho," the shuckers sang.

"Here is your corn ruler," General Thaddeus chanted.

"Oh ho ho ho ho ho ho ho," the shuckers sang again, and the work began.

The slaves laughed and joked as they worked furiously, tearing open the corn husks. The air filled with shucks. Ears of corn flew from the slaves' hands, arcing into the corn cribs. Nathaniel threw a corn cob. Jess ducked.

Then, triumphantly shucking the last ear of corn, Nathaniel sang, "Round up, double up, round up corn."

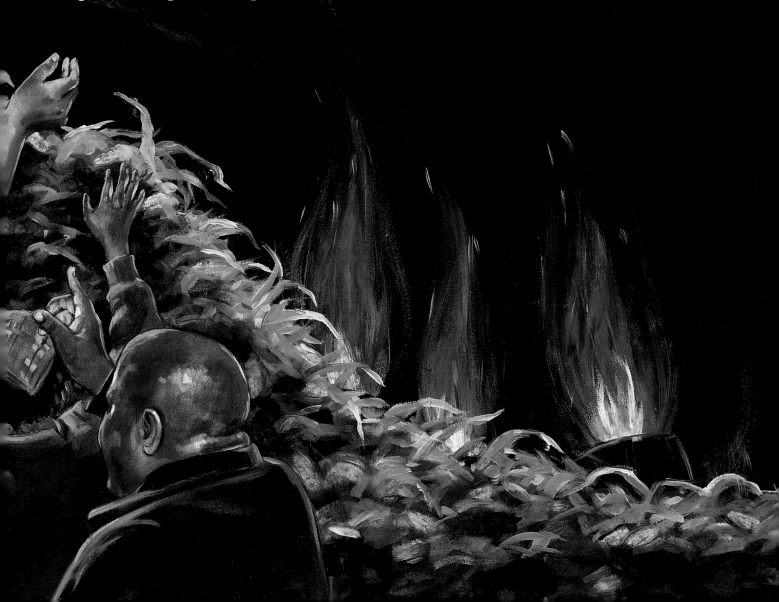

But Corn General Thaddeus, on the bigger pile, was declared winner. It was time to eat. Smiling, Jess grabbed a slice of pie.

Old Fiddler arrived, derby hat perched. Coal black, the old Affykin carried himself like a prince. He sat while his food and drink were brought.

At last, Fiddler stood up. He carved a circle in the dirt with his foot. "The toughest rassling boy will be strawbeater tonight," he said.

Nathaniel tossed down his coat. "I can fling any you boys ter inches from de ground."

Jess took a deep breath, clenched his fists, and entered the ring. Nathaniel laughed. He picked Jess up and flung him so hard Sis Wisa gasped.

Jess fell hard. He staggered up, his head sore. "I won't give up," he whispered.

"Seeing how you's so mannish," Nathaniel jeered, "I'll give you one more fall just to gives you the satisfaction." He took hold of Jess and flung him clean over his shoulder.

Jess fell hard again. He staggered up, grunting, "Ohhhh!" But then he whispered, "I won't give up. I will be strawbeater!" He grabbed hold of Nathaniel and wouldn't let go. Nathaniel jerked and twisted, but Jess held on. No matter how Nathaniel pushed and pulled, he couldn't break Jess's grip. Jess held on and on, and he held out. Finally someone in the crowd yelled, "Can we git to the dancin'?"

Fiddler grinned and said, "Strawbeater Jess lets the jig begin."
A skyrocket was thrown.

"I jarred him," Nathaniel protested as everyone marched
toward the dance.

Those who could not get seats for the dancing took their stand outside, peeping in the door and through the cabin's logs. Jess held out his straws and beat on the fiddle, *Tum tee tum, tum tee tum.* Fiddler called out:

*"Gentlemen to the right.
He carries a broad row, weeds out everything,
Hoes de corn, digs the taters.
Molly, see how she shake herself."*

Sis Wisa had joined the ladies quilting.

The dance over, Jess ran to his mother. "Mama, I was straw-beater."

"What a blessing, Strawbeater Jess," Sis Wisa said, tenderly touching his face.

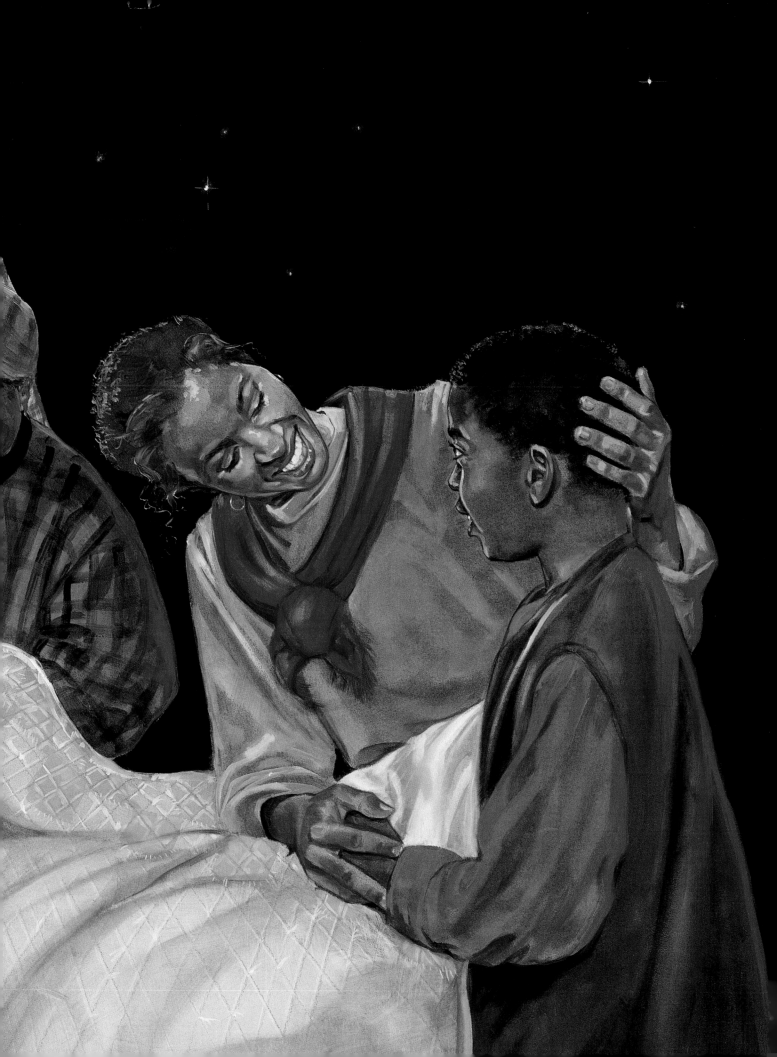

Sis Wisa, Jess, Nathaniel, and the other slaves from their farm started the walk home. A voice rang out, "Run, slave, run. The patrollers gonna get you." Jess's eyes were nearly shut. Sis Wisa gently hiked her manchild onto her back.